Abigail

Wheeler!

A story by Hans Manz retold by Ruth Cavin
with pictures by Werner Hofmann

A Here-and-There Book from Harlin Quist

Published by Harlin Quist, Incorporated.
Published simultaneously in the British Commonwealth by Quist Publishing, Limited.
Library of Congress Catalogue Card Number: 77-125504.
SBN: Trade / 8252-0098-9; Library / 8252-0999-7.
Copyright © 1969 by Diogenes Verlag AG, Zurich.
English text copyright © 1971 by Harlin Quist, Incorporated.

Before Mutti and Putti got to be Wheeler's parents, they spent their days just like everyone else. Well, *almost* like everyone else...

Putti was a chimney sweep. He had a ladder, several long and dirty brushes, and some funny-looking metal rods and hoops. He went from one house to another on his bicycle, climbing up into the chimneys and sweeping the soot from inside them. As he worked, a lot of the soot fell on him. But Putti didn't care.

Mutti didn't care, either. She didn't even care that Putti didn't wash the soot off right away when he came home. Putti usually ran up the stairs, burst through the door (he often tripped on the doorsill!) and rushed to the little balcony outside their attic window. There, while everyone else was eating dinner and reading the newspaper, Putti would spend the evening sailing paper airplanes.

Mutti enjoyed the evenings with her husband. She would sit on the balcony, eating plums and watching the airplanes sailing down, down over the rooftops to the street below.

"Whee!" Putti would shout, "Watch that one go!" The people in the village, looking up at them, remarked, "Paper planes and plum pits! What an odd pair!"

But things had to change, because Wheeler was waiting to be born.

One evening, Putti came running up the stairs in a swirl of soot, shouting, "Good evening, good Mutti; good evening, good wife! Get out the plums and the paper, because here comes Putti, the greatest paper plane flier of them all!" And he tripped over the doorsill and fell on his face.

"Not tonight," Mutti said as she helped him up.

"Why not?" Putti tried to dust himself off, but since he was dustier than the floor to begin with, it all seemed quite useless.

"Because we have to find a house," said Mutti. "We're going to have a baby soon, and this attic room is too small for three."

"A baby? Whee!" Putti took Mutti by the waist and swung her around as though he was going to sail *her* over the balcony.

Then he went out and got the beer can that was their bank.

Putti counted the coins – which was easy, since there were only three. In addition, there were five buttons, two paper clips and a small brown spider. The spider scurried away and hid.

Putti put the buttons and the paper clips back in the bank, keeping the three coins in his hand. "We can't buy even a tiny house with this," he said.

"I know," Mutti said. "Let's move first! Then we'll find a house later."

"What a clever idea!" Putti exclaimed. "Much better than the other way around!"

So the next morning they piled their belongings into a little cart and moved.

But they had no place to move to – which was troublesome.
Not for Mutti, however. "Let's go to sleep," she said.
"It's nighttime. By morning we'll have thought of something."

Putti was grateful to have such a clever wife, and he pulled
the bed out of the wagon. Mutti put the sheets and blankets on
it, and they went peacefully to sleep.

While they were sleeping, a lucky thing happened: the school
burned down. By morning, it was nothing but a heap of sooty
bricks and stones.

"Hoorah!" Putti shouted, looking at the mess. "Perfect to build
a house with!"

"I knew we'd think of something!" Mutti cried.

They found a field full of flowers, weeds, chickens and some

worn-out cars that people had dumped there. Mutti particularly liked an old red truck with white curtains in the windows, even though it had no engine. A truck with curtains was *very* special!

There was lots of space in the field for their new house. Putti went to work.

The house was a little strange. In fact, it looked more like a patchwork quilt than a house. The first load of bricks came from the burned school house. They were black from the fire. Putti started with them.

On the way back for more, he found some nice brown stones. "Why not?" he asked himself. "I won't have to pull them as far." So the house became a black and brown one.

All of the schoolboys, without a school to go to, stood around watching Putti. "How about some red bricks?" one of them asked. "I know where to find lots of them." So Putti finished up the walls in red.

"White on the top!" called out Mutti, who came down the road with a load of tools she had borrowed from the neighbors. "It's got to have white on top, like snow on a mountain."
Putti painted the grey shingles on the roof white.
Finally, the house was finished.
Mutti put the furniture in. "Putti! There's no place for the baby to sleep!"

They went into the village to shop. Their favorite store belonged to the Collector.

As a young man, the Collector had picked up trash for the village. Often, he would find treasures that other people simply didn't care about. One week it would be an alarm clock that stopped ticking; another week, a chicken coop; the third, something really wonderful, like a totem pole. He kept what he liked. And, after a while, he had quite a collection. So he opened a store with his odds-and-ends.

He didn't have a cradle, however, or even a crib. "How about some soup plates?" he asked Mutti.
But she didn't see how a baby could sleep in them.
"A large dog house, perhaps? Upside down it might do...
A snug warm tepee?"

Mutti shook her head. Nothing seemed right. She couldn't say exactly what *would* be right, but she knew that babies are seldom happy in dog houses or tepees – not to mention soup plates!

The next day, Putti didn't come home until very late. While Mutti was waiting for him, she climbed into her favorite red truck – the one with the white curtains.

When Putti arrived, he was pushing a curious package, all wrapped up in brown paper. "Mutti!" he called out. "Where are you? I have a surprise!"

"So have I!" Mutti answered.

And Putti looked through the window in the truck.

"Whee!" he shouted. "Hoorah!"

In the back of the truck was Mutti, with a brand new baby boy! Putti kissed her. Then he kissed the baby boy. Then he shouted a few more times.

When he had calmed down a bit, Mutti asked, "What's *your* surprise?"

Putti tore the paper off of the strange package.

"A buggy!" said Mutti. "And just right for a baby bed too!"

They wheeled the carriage into the house, with the new baby in it. "He's beautiful!" Mutti sighed. "And he's ours!" Putti added.

All babies cry sometimes; it's the only way they can talk. But this baby cried at the oddest times. He also *stopped* crying at the oddest times!

When Mutti lifted him out of the buggy, he howled.

"Give him to me," Putti said. He took the baby, and the baby howled some more.

"Give him back," Mutti said. She took the baby, and the baby screamed.

"Let me take him again," Putti said. With the baby in his arms, he sat down in the big chair that had belonged to his great, great grandfather. In fact, it was their *only* chair; and it was so old that it had little wheels on the legs, which helped Mutti a great deal when she dusted the floor.

The baby stopped crying; he gurgled. "See?" said Putti proudly.

Mutti took the baby from him, to give him his nightly bath. The baby howled. "See?" said Putti again.

The baby cried all during his bath; he cried while he was being dried and powdered and diapered and fed. But when Mutti put him in the buggy, he hiccupped and then smiled. He was happy again.

Mutti and Putti were confused. They called the Doctor.

When the Doctor took the baby, he screamed. And while the Doctor was poking and thumping him, the baby howled until he was red in the face.

"He's fine," the Doctor said—though he had to shout to be heard above the screaming.

Across the field, Miss Myrtle and Miss Maud listened to the screaming and the shouting. Glump and Blump, their two sour bulldogs, growled in horror.

"That's what you get when you have odd people living near you," Miss Myrtle said to Miss Maud in a vinegary voice. "They build a strange house–all different colors! Next thing you know they start having babies in an old truck! And right after that comes squalling and caterwauling and wailing till you can't hear a bulldog bark!"

"What, sister Myrtle?" asked Miss Maud. "I can't hear you with all this noise!"

"Grrr," growled Glump.

"Rrrruf," barked Blump.

In the little house, all had grown quiet. The baby was sleeping peacefully in his carriage, and Putti was deep in thought.

"He's all right now," Putti said.

"He's always all right when he's in the carriage," Mutti said.

Putti began to jump up and down. "Whee!" he yelled. "Listen, Mutti! He's all right in the big carriage. And he's all right in the big chair. And he was all right in the truck. Mutti, he likes to be on wheels! He cries when he's not! Watch!"

Putti brought in his sooty bicycle, and then picked up the baby. The little baby face started to twist; the baby mouth opened to howl.

"No, you don't!" cried Mutti, and popped him onto the bike.

"Gloop!" said the baby happily.

Mutti looked at Putti with admiration. "Putti, you are the smartest man in the world! Of course that's it! He's only happy when he's on wheels!"

"We'll name him *Wheeler!*" Putti cried. "Look! he's laughing!"

And Mutti and Putti started laughing too–*and* dancing *and* singing. Loudly.

Next door, Miss Myrtle sniffed to Miss Maud with a sour apple sniff: "When the baby isn't making the air hideous with noise, his parents are!"

"We must have him christened, now that we have a name for him," Mutti said. "Right away, so we can call him Wheeler for real."

"But he'll scream and cry the whole time! I don't know if the Pastor will like that."

"Let's go see him," Mutti said.

The Pastor was the best person in the village for them to talk to about this. He was on wheels most of the time himself, roaring around the village on his old motorcycle. When Mutti and Putti came into the churchyard, he was tinkering with the engine.

"We'd like to have our new baby christened next Sunday," Putti explained.

"Fine!" said the Pastor. "What name?"

"Wheeler!" Mutti told him.

"Excellent," said the Pastor, patting his old cycle. "A good name! Odd, which I like...And does he wheel?"

"Well, in a manner of speaking" said Mutti shyly. "You tell him, Putti."

So Putti told the Pastor about the crying.

The Pastor was delighted. He liked a good, hard problem. "Leave it to me," he said.

After Mutti and Putti left, he thought for a while, riding slowly and noisily around the churchyard. Then he went up to his attic. His curious cat came, too, and watched as he practiced with a toy he hadn't taken out since he was a boy.

That Sunday, Mutti and Putti left the baby outside the church in his carriage and went in. Mutti was a little nervous. After all, the whole village was there: the Collector, the Innkeeper, the Doctor, Miss Myrtle and Miss Maud — everybody. (Except the bulldogs.)

When the Pastor came out to conduct the service, an astonished buzz went through the room.

"He's grown at least half a foot taller since last week!" the Collector said to the Innkeeper in an astonished whisper.

"Nonsense!" hissed the Innkeeper. "People as old as the Pastor don't grow taller!"

But he certainly *looked* taller.

"Look how he moves," whispered Miss Maud to Miss Myrtle. "He seems to glide along!"

"Don't be a donkey!" Miss Myrtle answered. But the Pastor seemed to glide along.

After the service came the christening. Mutti waited nervously while Putti ran down to the carriage and got the baby. Back he raced, and threw the baby into the Pastor's arms just as the little mouth opened to howl.

Everyone watched and waited, expecting the worst.

But the baby didn't howl. He smiled. He smiled all through the christening, and when the Pastor got to the end, the baby laughed out loud! Mutti was so startled she dropped her handkerchief.

She stooped to pick it up, and that's how she found out the Pastor's secret. Hidden by his long robes, but sticking out enough for Mutti to see, were a pair of roller skates!

A year went by, and the chimney sweep's little family were very happy. Putti cleaned chimneys; Mutti took care of Wheeler. She fed him and bathed him and played with him and always saw to it that he was on wheels. (Putti had even fixed wheels to the tin bathtub.)

Sometimes Putti took Wheeler with him for company while he swept chimneys. It made a nice change for the little boy. And so Wheeler grew, and things were very pleasant. The people in the village got used to Putti's funny house and funny ways. The sour old sisters, Miss Myrtle and Miss Maud, couldn't find anything to complain about.

Glump and Blump couldn't find anything to growl about but they growled anyhow. Dogs don't need reasons.

Until the time came that Wheeler was old enough to walk.

By that time
he could talk a little.

Mutti set him on the floor.

"Wheeler won't walk!"
he shouted—and sat down.

Putti tried cutting a hole in the bottom of the little cart. "He can sit in here, and walk and wheel at the same time," he said.

"Putti, how clever you are!" Mutti murmured.

They put Wheeler into the cart.

"Wheeler won't walk!" Wheeler yelled, pulling his feet up out of the hole.

The wagon started to roll. Mutti and Putti watched horrified as it rolled faster, faster, faster down the hill...and wham!
Right into Miss Myrtle's and Miss Maud's fence!
Up from behind the fence came two sour faces, like two jack-in-the-boxes. They had been gardening in that exact spot.

Glump and Blump yelped. "Yipe! yipe! yipe!"

"Chatter, chatter, chatter!" "Scold, scold, scold!"

Wheeler simply smiled. "Wheeler just wheels," he told them.
"Wheeler won't walk. Bye-bye!"

"Well," said Putti to Mutti. "That's the way it is. Wheeler won't walk and Wheeler wants to wheel. We'd better get him something that he can steer." And he went to the Collector, who tried to sell him a set of matched soup plates.

"No," said Putti firmly, and bought Wheeler a blue tricycle.

Soon Wheeler was the best tricyclist in town. He could go faster than Putti on his bike. He could go faster than the Pastor on his motorcycle.

That was the beginning of a wild time for the village. Wheeler rode his tricycle all day. Through the Baker's shop, back and forth past the pastries and bread loaves. Wheee! Wheee!

"Watch out for Wheeler!" yelled Wheeler. "Watch out for my wheels!"

"Why don't you walk?" roared the Baker.

In and out of the butcher shop, Wheeler whirled, scaring the cat, scattering sawdust over everything.

"Get out of my store!" roared the Butcher. "Why won't you walk?"

Screeeech! With a squeal of brakes, Wheeler stopped his tricycle by the shoemaker's shop, and stuck his feet in the shoemaker's cellar window. "Fix my shoes!" he cried. "Mutti said for you to fix my shoes!"

"How can I fix your shoes through the window while you sit on that tricycle?" grumbled the Shoemaker. "Walk! Walk! Walk down the steps and bring them in through the door."

But Wheeler wouldn't walk.

He rode, though. He rode around the village, picking up things he found. He raced in and out of barnyards, frightening the animals into squawks and moos of terror. He chased all the pigs into the center of town, where they ran up against the Lawyer and the Doctor and the Innkeeper, and pushed those stuffy men around the village square.

Everybody was furious at Wheeler! "Why doesn't the chimney sweep do something about that boy?" they asked one another.

They were so angry they hired a different chimney sweep.

He was a sad-faced man who came pedaling slowly into the village each morning from a town far away. By the time he arrived, he was so hungry that he spent the rest of the day eating. The chimneys got very dirty, and they had to call Putti back to clean them.

(Putti was a very good chimney sweep. You could tell by his face. With all the soot that was on his face and his clothes and his brushes, surely there couldn't have been much left in the chimney.)

Putti and Mutti didn't mind any of this. They were very happy. On Sundays, Putti took the whole family riding. He'd tie the little cart to the back of his bicycle, and Mutti sat in it (keeping her feet well away from the hole Putti had made). Wheeler was tied on at the end on his blue tricycle. Putti would start up, and they'd race through the streets of the village. Everybody ran when they saw those three coming!

Putti liked to swing around corners without slowing down. Mutti whipped around behind him, and Wheeler, being at the tail end, swung fastest and hardest of all. Anyone unlucky enough to be in the way just got knocked over.

Then, to make matters worse, the Pastor bought a new motorcycle–and gave his old one to Putti.
Mutti and Putti made a sidecar for Wheeler out of his bathtub.

Now they could ride even faster–and with a lot more noise–
all around the village. Wheeler had put the whole family
on wheels!

Everyone in the village (except the Pastor) talked a lot about
the odd chimney sweep and his terrible little boy.

At last, the end came. Wheeler had zoomed into the bakery,
upset a shelf of cakes, and left the baker covered with icing.
He'd zoomed into the Butcher's and left the Butcher tangled
and tied in a long rope of sausages.
He'd put his foot through the Shoemaker's closed window.
He left the Shoemaker grumblingly sweeping up broken glass.
Then he'd flashed back home on his blue tricycle.

Soon Mutti and Putti and Wheeler saw a cloud of dust moving
in the road. "Here come all the villagers!" Mutti cried.
"Let's hide!" said Putti.

Mutti ran into
the old red truck.
Putti crouched down
under the hood.
And Wheeler –
of course,
Wheeler wrapped
himself around
the wheel.

When the villagers got there, they couldn't find anyone. There were many more cars and trucks dumped here now, and the plants and weeds had grown tall, and the chickens squawked and upset people. They looked and looked, while Mutti and Putti and Wheeler tried not to giggle. But they couldn't find anyone. They were stopped in their search by the Lawyer, who hissed at them. When he had their attention, he pointed. Right to Wheeler's blue tricycle.

Then he put his finger to his lips, and motioned for them to come away. "I guess we'd better give up," he said in a loud voice. "They're not here."

"But..." began the Collector.

The Lawyer put his fingers to his lips again. "Let's go," he said, and began walking down the road. Puzzled, they followed him.

As soon as they were around a bend in the road, where they couldn't be seen or heard by anyone at Wheeler's house, he told them his plan. "Tonight, when they're all asleep, we'll go back," he said, "and we'll *take away his tricycle!* He won't walk," he explained to them. "He only wheels. Without the tricycle, he'll have nothing to wheel *on!* Then he'll have to stay home, and not bother us!"

"What a good trick!" the Collector said. "What a clever man you are, Lawyer!"

All the villagers agreed. "*That* will stop that boy!" the Innkeeper said.

Only sour old Miss Myrtle and Miss Maud weren't altogether satisfied. "You mark my word, sister," said Miss Myrtle to Miss Maud. "They still won't settle down to being ordinary people. What can you expect from the sort who live in the middle of a heap of old cars? And have their babies in trucks! Humph!" Miss Myrtle, it was plain to see, didn't plan on having any babies in a truck.

Mutti and Putti and Wheeler had watched the villagers leave. They came out of their hiding places. "Whee!" shouted Putti. "We outsmarted them! Let's celebrate with a picnic!" So that night they had dinner in one of the cars. Sour old Miss Maud and Miss Myrtle watched from their window and clucked. "Disgraceful!" they said. And "Unsanitary!"

Very late that night, the villagers gathered in the square, and very, very quietly, set out for Wheeler's house. The little house was dark – Mutti and Putti and Wheeler were sound asleep. Softly, the Lawyer and the Collector tiptoed in among the cars. The blue tricycle was sitting right where they had seen it that afternoon. Carefully, the Collector picked it up...

The Lawyer found Mutti and Putti's beer can on the doorstep of the little house. Each villager put a nickel into it, so as not to be stealing the tricycle. Then they went softly back to their houses.

The Collector put the tricycle carefully in the back room of his shop. "That boy won't get this back in a hurry!" he said. And he laughed wickedly: "Heh! Heh! Heh!"

Early the next morning, the shopkeepers opened their shops, feeling safe from the wheels of the blue tricycle for the first time in many months.

As the morning went by, the villagers gathered in the square to congratulate one another on their clever trick.

The Lawyer was treating everyone to coffee and buns when the Collector happened to look down the road. He was amazed to see Miss Maud and Miss Myrtle running toward the square as fast as their bony legs would carry them. They looked quite undignified. Behind them stumped Glump and Blump, panting and wheezing.

"Look out!" shrieked Miss Myrtle. And Miss Maud echoed, "Look out! Look out!"

"What is it? What's the matter? What's wrong?"

They pointed long quivering fingers down the road, the way they had just come.

And the whole village saw Wheeler. Down the road he came, faster than any tricycle, faster than his father's bicycle, faster than the Pastor's motorcycle. He was a whirling, swirling shape, and they all knew that to get anywhere near that would be like walking into a whirlwind.

Down the road came Wheeler. He wasn't walking! He was certainly not walking! Without a tricycle or a cart or anything else, he was *wheeling* down the road. Somersaulting, cartwheeling, somersaulting again, and then doing *three* cartwheels at a time. Wheeler had found a way to wheel without wheels!

"There's no winning with Wheeler," everyone sighed. "He's got the best of us!"

And they all agreed that the Collector should give the blue tricycle back to Wheeler.

Which he did.

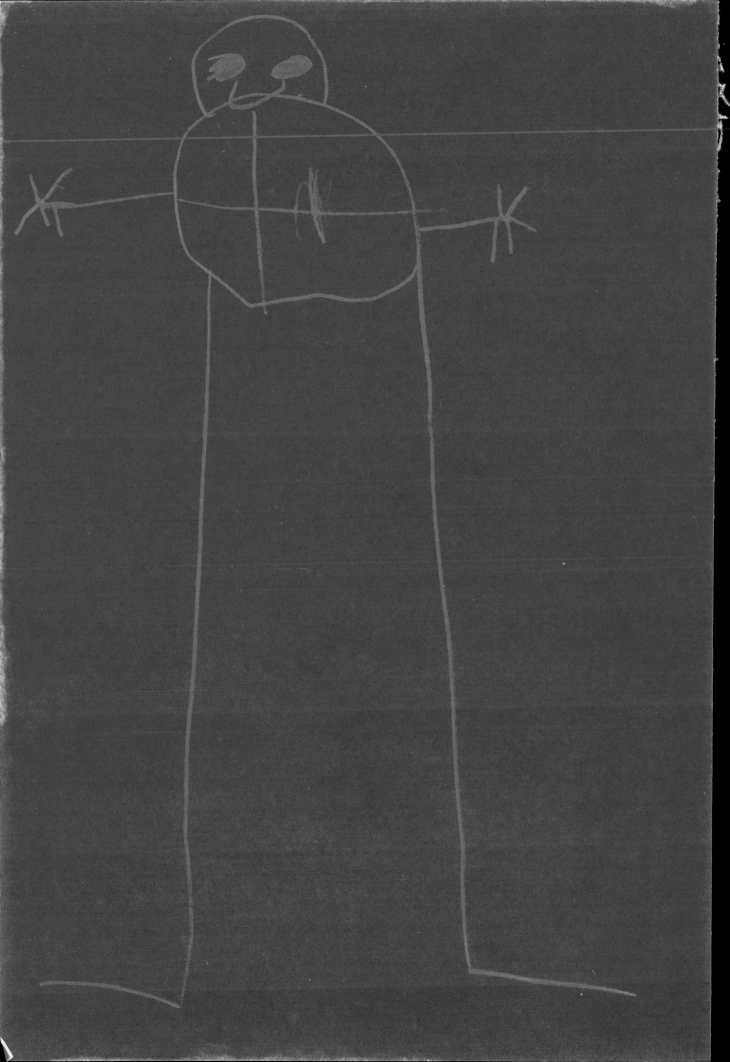